Under the Sleepy Stars

Under the Sleepy Stars

by Stephanie Shaw
Illustrated by Rebecca Harry

SCHOLASTIC INC.

In the still of the forest
the animals rest,
While Owl and her owlet
look down from their nest.

Little Owlet keeps watch
with his wide-awake eyes
As all go to sleep
beneath darkening skies.

"Mama, who settles Fawn
    in her bed for the night?"
"Her mama, my Owlet,
    will tuck her in tight."

"Mama, who sings a song
until Mouse falls asleep?"
"The crickets sing high notes.
The bullfrogs sing deep."

There's a whisper of wind,
and the branch gently swings,
As Owlet peeks out from
his mama's warm wings.

"Mama, what if the bunnies
are scared of the night?"
"The star-sprinkled sky
will provide a soft light."

"Mama, what if Cub needs
a kiss and a hug?"
"His mama, dear Owlet,
will make sure he is snug."

Now the animals sleep,
as the moon shines above,

All wrapped in the warmth
of their own mama's love.

Soon night slips away
and the sun starts to rise;
Mama rocks little Owlet
as he closes his eyes.

"Mama, who do you love
the way those mamas do?"
"My sweet, precious Owlet,
I'll always love you."

In memory of my mother-in-law, Sarah Longfellow. With love
~ S. S.

For my babies, Willow and Iolo xxxx
~ R. H.

Originally published in Great Britain in 2015 by Little Tiger Press Ltd

No part of this publication may be reproduced, stored in a retrieval system, or transmitted in any form or by any means, electronic, mechanical, photocopying, recording, or otherwise, without written permission of the publisher. For information regarding permission, write to Tiger Tales, an imprint of Little Tiger Press Ltd, 1 The Coda Centre, 189 Munster Road, London, England SW6 6AW.

ISBN 978-0-545-89055-7

12 11 10 9 8 7 6 5 4 3   17 18 19 20/0

Printed in the U.S.A.   40

First Scholastic printing, October 2015